Where Does It Come From?

From Garden to Pickle

by Penelope S. Nelson

Bullfrog Books

Ideas for Parents and Teachers

Bullfrog Books let children practice reading informational text at the earliest reading levels. Repetition, familiar words, and photo labels support early readers.

Before Reading

- Discuss the cover photo. What does it tell them?
- Look at the picture glossary together. Read and discuss the words.

Read the Book

- "Walk" through the book and look at the photos. Let the child ask questions. Point out the photo labels.
- Read the book to the child, or have him or her read independently.

After Reading

- Prompt the child to think more. Ask: Do you eat pickles? Did you know pickles were cucumbers before you read this book?

Bullfrog Books are published by Jump!
5357 Penn Avenue South
Minneapolis, MN 55419
www.jumplibrary.com

Library of Congress Cataloging-in-Publication Data

Names: Nelson, Penelope, 1994– author.
Title: From garden to pickle / Penelope S. Nelson.
Description: Minneapolis: Jump!, Inc., [2021]
Series: Where does it come from?
Audience: Ages 5–8.
Identifiers: LCCN 2019053327 (print)
LCCN 2019053328 (ebook)
ISBN 9781645275350 (library binding)
ISBN 9781645275367 (paperback)
ISBN 9781645275374 (ebook)
Subjects: LCSH: Pickles—Juvenile literature.
Cucumbers—Preservation—Juvenile literature.
Canning and preserving—Juvenile literature.
Classification: LCC TX805 .N45 2021 (print)
LCC TX805 (ebook) | DDC 641.4/62—dc23
LC record available at https://lccn.loc.gov/2019053327
LC ebook record available at https://lccn.loc.gov/2019053328

Editor: Jenna Gleisner
Designer: Anna Peterson

Photo Credits: Nataliia Melnychuk/Shutterstock, cover; Africa Studio/Shutterstock, 1, 12; Sever180/Shutterstock, 3; Lapina/Shutterstock, 4; Lyubov Demus/Dreamstime, 5; Tatevosian Yana/Shutterstock, 6–7, 22tl; RossHelen/Shutterstock, 8–9, 22tr, 23bl; Ingrid Heczko/Dreamstime, 10–11; Verena Joy/Shutterstock, 13 (background); Claire Lucia/Shutterstock, 13 (foreground); Alexlukin/Shutterstock, 14–15, 16–17, 22br, 23tr; GarysFRP/iStock, 18, 22bm, 23tl; Jupiterimages/Getty, 19, 23br; RuslanDashinsky/iStock, 20–21, 22bl; domnitsky/Shutterstock, 24.

Printed in the United States of America at Corporate Graphics in North Mankato, Minnesota.

Table of Contents

Crunchy Snacks

Cam loves pickles!

Where do they come from?

Gardens!

They start
as cucumbers.

Cool!

We pick them when they are small.

We scrub them.

Why?

To get the dirt off.

We put them in jars.

We add garlic.
We add dill.

They grow in our garden, too!

Nice!

brine

We make a brine.

We pour it in.

Then we screw
on each lid.

Ready to go!

lid

The jars go in a pot.
Water boils.

The lids seal!

Neat!

We wait a few weeks.

We eat some!

Crunch!

From Garden to Table

How do dill pickles get to our tables?

1. We pick cucumbers from a garden.

2. We scrub the cucumbers to get dirt off.

3. We put them in jars with garlic, dill, and brine. We screw on the lids.

4. We boil the jars in a pot of water until they seal.

5. Weeks later, we eat pickles!

Picture Glossary

boils
Heats to the point where it bubbles.

brine
A liquid mixture of water and other ingredients, such as vinegar and salt.

scrub
To clean something by rubbing or brushing it hard.

seal
To shut, fasten, or close something up tight.

Index

To Learn More

Finding more information is as easy as 1, 2, 3.

1. Go to www.factsurfer.com
2. Enter "fromgardentopickle" into the search box.
3. Choose your book to see a list of websites.